Cindy Jefferies

USBORNE

For my lovely sister Rachael

First published in 2007 by Usborne Publishing Ltd., Usborne House,
83-85 Saffron Hill, London EC1N 8RT, England. www.usborne.com

A CIP catalogue record for this book is available from the British Library.

JF AMJJASOND/07

ISBN 9780746073049

Printed in Great Britain.

Glamour! * Talent!

* Stardom! *

* Fame and fortune *
could be one step away!

Welcome to

Fame
School

For another fix of

read

Reach for the Stars

Rising Star

Secret Ambition

Rivals!

Tara's Triumph

Lucky Break

Solo Star

Christmas Stars

Coming soon...

Battle of the Bands

1 New Term

The temperature was well below freezing when Pop and Lolly got out of the car. Although the sun was shining, it didn't have any warmth in it. It had been chilly before Christmas, but now in January it was deep midwinter. Lolly grabbed her scarf and wrapped it around her head to protect her face from the bitter wind. The identical twins were stiff after their journey and felt glad to have arrived back at Rockley Park School. It was a new term and it was always fun catching up with all their friends.

"I'll see if I can find a trolley for our luggage," said Pop, crunching over the mixture of salt and grit that had been spread liberally all over the path. Last term

Pop Diva

Judge Jim, the Head of the Rock Department, had fallen on the ice and broken his ankle. No doubt Mrs. Sharkey wanted to make sure there wouldn't be any more accidents like that this term.

Pop made her way carefully indoors to where the housemistress was welcoming her boarders.

"Watch out!" Mrs. Pinto warned, as Pop wheeled the luggage trolley awkwardly out of the building, narrowly missing her housemistress's toes.

"Sorry!" Pop called, stifling a giggle.

It didn't take long to push Pop's heavy cases along the corridor and into the girls' room. Being on the ground floor was cool because they were near the kitchen, the sitting room and the room where the house computers were kept.

Pop and Lolly went back outside to collect Lolly's luggage and say goodbye to their parents. Rockley Park was a boarding school and the girls wouldn't see their family again for a few weeks. It was always a bit sad saying goodbye, but there was so much to look forward to that they didn't really mind. As well as the usual lessons, Rockley Park taught its students all about the music business. The school was full of talented pupils who were determined to realize their dreams of becoming successful singers, dancers, recording engineers or any one of the other jobs to be found in the industry.

"Come on!" urged Pop, after they'd waved goodbye. "Let's see who else is here. I didn't notice Chloe's or Tara's luggage, so maybe they haven't arrived yet."

"We ought to hang our dresses up," said Lolly, "or they'll get creased." Pop and Lolly always had loads of clothes with them because they were famous models and loved to dress up, but Pop wasn't as good as Lolly at remembering to look after them.

"You're right," agreed Pop. "Let's do that first." They'd wheeled Lolly's cases halfway down the corridor when a yell came from behind them.

"Hey!" It was one of their roommates, Chloe Tompkins.

"So you *have* arrived," said Lolly, with a smile for her

best friend. "We didn't think you had."

"Hi, Chloe! How are you?" Pop called. "Did you see our interview?"

"Of course! It was brilliant," Chloe said. "Thanks for phoning me. I could easily have missed it. And is it true what you said on TV?" she went on. "*Do* you have a record deal?"

"Yes! It's *so* exciting." Pop squeezed past the trolley so she could give Chloe a huge hug. Lolly did the same. It was great to see Chloe again.

"I'm sorry. We weren't allowed to tell *anyone* about the deal until it was announced on TV," Lolly told Chloe apologetically. "But we didn't want you to miss the programme."

"That's okay." Chloe smiled. "It was really exciting hearing about it that way. Did you get my text?"

"Yes, thanks. And we saw *your* programme, too," Lolly told Chloe. "You made a wonderful Rising Star."

At the end of every school year, Rockley Park was invited to send its best students to perform a special Rising Stars Concert at the local TV station, and Chloe had been one of them. Although the programme was recorded at the end of the summer term, it wasn't transmitted until Christmas, so it had been a long wait for Chloe to see herself on television.

"Thanks," said Chloe with a grin. "But the concert was ages ago, and your record contract is really hot news. How did it happen?"

Several girls appeared from other bedrooms. They gathered round and added their voices to the chaos. Then Mrs. Pinto appeared and clapped her hands for silence.

"Girls! Girls! Stop cluttering up the hallway. Other people are trying to get in, and someone else wants the trolley, Pop. Don't just abandon it. Take it straight back outside when you've finished. Then, if you must squeal and shriek, go and do that on the way to tea."

Pop was aware of several of the younger students watching her and Lolly with eyes like saucers. Of course, they probably hadn't met anyone with a record contract before! Pop shot them a beaming, celebrity smile. Meanwhile, Chloe struggled along the corridor clutching an assortment of carrier bags.

Once Pop, Lolly and Chloe were all in their room together, with their luggage, Pop sank down onto her bed with a satisfied sigh.

"Have you really got a record deal?" It was Jade, a tall, blonde girl who was in the year above. The year nine rooms were in the opposite corridor but the twins' news had spread to all three years in Paddock House. Soon, a large group of girls had gathered in the doorway.

"Yes, they have," Jade's roommate, Betsy, told her. "Didn't you see them on TV over Christmas?"

Jade shook her head.

"Poppy Lowther!" The crowd of girls round the door parted and Mrs. Pinto appeared looking very cross. "I told you to bring the luggage trolley straight back. What will the younger students think of such unhelpfulness? And you older girls don't belong here," she added, glaring at Jade and the other girls. "If you want to natter in a big group, go into the common room."

The year nines melted away, and Mrs. Pinto directed her gaze back to Pop.

"Sorry, Mrs. Pinto." Pop had jumped guiltily to her feet. "We were just talking about our TV interview last weekend." She hesitated. "And our record deal."

Mrs. Pinto didn't look impressed.

"There's no room for any prima donnas here, as you very well know," she reminded Pop. "You and Lolly have never let your modelling success go to your heads, so I hope you won't let an appearance on television spoil you. You're here to work hard, not swan around like empty-headed starlets."

"Sorry," said Pop again, feeling rather ashamed. It was her exuberance rather than any big-headedness taking over, but Mrs. Pinto wasn't going to give her the benefit of the doubt.

"It's up to you to set an example to the younger ones," Mrs. Pinto continued in a milder voice, speaking to all three girls. "You know how it can go to your head just to have won a place here. You lot have to be sober and sensible about any success you have, don't you?"

Pop Diva

The girls nodded. No one was encouraged to get big-headed at Rockley Park. The music business was notoriously fickle and although every student dreamed of getting a break, it didn't do to become complacent.

Pop and Lolly had been well-known child models for years, but their agent had been at pains to make them realize that sooner or later the fashion industry would lose interest in the Lowther twins. That was why they had decided to attend Rockley Park. If they could capitalize on their name and become pop stars as well, they would be able to extend their careers. So far, it looked as if the idea was working.

"We still need to sort our things out," Lolly remembered. "And can I swap with you this term, Pop, and have the bed by the window?"

Mrs. Pinto smiled. "That sounds more like the Lowther twins I know," she said. "And once you've finished unpacking, do go and have your tea."

"Okay," they agreed.

"And Pop..."

"Yes?"

"I watched the television interview too," said Mrs. Pinto. "You spoke very well and the record contract is a real achievement. Well done, both of you!"

As Mrs. Pinto left, the last of Pop and Lolly's roommates appeared, pulling an expensive-looking black case on wheels. It was Tara Fitzgerald, wearing her usual serious expression on a very pale face.

Pop looked at her expectantly. She had sent Tara a text, telling her that the twins were going to be on TV. Surely she had watched the programme? But Tara didn't seem inclined to talk. After giving them all a swift hello, she unzipped her suitcase and proceeded to take out a pile of the black tops and jeans she always wore, adding them to the others in her cupboard.

"Hi, Tara," said Chloe. "Have you heard Pop and Lolly's news?"

Tara smiled slightly, but didn't reply. She had an infuriating ability to remain silent for ages.

"I bet you have," Chloe teased. "Pop told me she'd texted you. You *must* have watched the programme. You always want to know everything that's going on."

Tara raised her eyebrows. "Do I?" she said.

Pop couldn't make up her mind whether Tara was simply trying to wind them up or really hadn't heard about the recording contract. She let an armful of shoes fall to the floor with a clatter. "Honestly!" she said. "Please tell us, Tara. Do you know what's happened or not?"

Tara looked thoughtful. She unpacked a photograph of her parents and then turned to look squarely at Pop.

"Don't tell me," she said. "I expect I can guess. This is the first day of term, isn't it? You've only been here for ten minutes and I bet you've been in trouble already!"

2 Teatime

Pop laughed ruefully. Trust Tara to give the wrong answer and yet still be right. "I don't mean that sort of thing!" she said. "You know me. I'm *never* in trouble!" she added with a grin. "No. We've got a record deal. The Lowther twins are going to release a single! How about that for news?"

Tara grunted and threw her coat onto the bed furthest from the door. "I saw the interview," she acknowledged. "I suppose you're going to go on about it all term, now?" She sighed, but then a slight smile twitched her usually deadpan expression. "Congratulations," she said at last. "It's what we're all here for, isn't it? So, well done. All right if I have this bed again?" she added, looking at Chloe. "I don't like being too near the door."

"Chloe was going to have it as you were last to arrive," said Lolly.

Tara took no notice. She put the photograph on the bedside table and added a paperback book. Pop looked over at Chloe, and Chloe shrugged. Pop considered standing up for her and rejected the idea. It wouldn't matter what anyone said. Tara usually got her own way and really there wasn't that much to choose between the beds.

The girls spent a few minutes longer unpacking. But by the time Pop had filled her wardrobe to bursting she was getting bored with the work. "Let's do like Mrs. Pinto said and go for tea," she suggested. "I'm *starving*."

"Me too," agreed Chloe, standing on tiptoe to put her empty suitcase on top of the wardrobe. "And I'm all unpacked anyway!"

The four girls made their way over to the main house. As soon as they got into the dining room, they spotted some of the boys from their year.

"Danny!"

"Ed!"

"Hi, Marmalade!" yelled Pop to a boy with long, corkscrew, ginger curls.

"Take cover!" Marmalade warned the boys at his table with a grin. "Girl alert!"

But really, everyone was pleased to see each other. There were hugs all round before the girls got something to eat, settled down at the boys' table and started to catch up with the gossip.

"Well." Pop cut up the cake on her plate and put her knife down with a clatter. "We're going to be making a single. It's so exciting that I might have to scream in a minute!" She put her hands to her ears and screwed up her face. The others winced, but all that came out was a little, excited squeak. Pop grinned broadly. "I can't wait to hear our song on the radio," she went on.

"I can't wait to find out what it will be!" said Lolly. "We don't know yet."

"Do you get to choose the song?" asked Marmalade.

"I'm not sure," said Pop. "All we know at the

moment is that we'll be recording several tracks. I suppose they'll choose the one that sounds best."

"Tell us how you got the contract," asked Chloe.

"Well, we hadn't realized that Satin, our agent, put some footage of us singing onto her website. You remember," said Lolly, "it was filmed at school last year."

"I remember," said Chloe. "I'll never forget it because I got to sing the chorus with you! It was brilliant."

Pop carried on the story. "Somebody in the record company saw the clip and phoned Satin up. The first we knew about it was our agent telling us that we were going to record a single this term. It's just what we hoped would happen. Who knows where it might lead!"

"To an album maybe!" suggested Chloe with shining eyes.

"Well, yes," agreed Pop. "Hopefully. Wouldn't that be amazing? There'll be more television appearances and goodness knows what else. We'll be branching out into other stuff as well."

"Maybe," said Lolly mildly. "But I don't suppose our star will shine for ever."

Pop frowned at her sister. Everyone knew that Lolly's plan was to train to be a doctor eventually, while Pop's ambition was to stay in the limelight for as long as possible.

"So what other ideas have you got?" asked Ed. "You're already models and now you're going to make a single. What other stuff could you possibly have decided to do?"

Ed had hit home with that remark. There weren't really any other ideas. Pop had just got a bit carried away and had exaggerated. She hesitated. To be making a single *was* the most amazing thing in her life, but her ambition didn't have to stop with that, did it? There must be loads of other starry things she could do. Then a thought struck her.

"Television presenting," she told Ed importantly. "I loved it when they interviewed us and I bet I could do it. Satin said ages ago that she thought I could be a good TV presenter. Maybe I could be a chat-show host!"

Tara looked scathing. "You don't have time to do that as well as everything else," she said. "Besides, who would give you a presenting slot on television? It's ridiculous."

"I *could* do it," argued Pop. "After all, I *am* quite well known already."

"Oh, please!" drawled Tara sarcastically. "Let's all hear it for our megastar, who hasn't even made her first recording yet."

Pop could see that Lolly felt embarrassed, but she didn't care. They *were* well known, and might as well make use of the fact. It didn't mean she was becoming big-headed. Then she noticed a couple of younger girls hovering nearby. "Can I help you?" she said to the nearest girl, who had curly brown hair.

The girls came closer and each held out a piece of paper. "Could we have your autograph?" the curly haired girl asked.

"What?" asked Pop, wondering if she had misheard.

"We'd like your autograph," explained the other girl, rummaging in her pocket and finding a gel pen. "And yours, of course," she added to Lolly, who was looking even more embarrassed.

"We saw you on telly recently and we know you're famous," the curly haired girl insisted, getting bolder by the moment. "I've seen you modelling clothes in my magazine as well."

"Please. We want your signatures before you make your first single. Then we can tell our friends we knew you first." The second girl, who had short, pale blonde hair looked very earnest. She held out her piece of paper so it nearly touched Pop's hand.

"The thing is," said Lolly awkwardly, "we're not supposed to encourage this sort of thing. We're no better than anyone else here, you know."

"That's right," said Tara. "You don't want to encourage Pop!"

Pop glared at Tara. She had been going to refuse too, but now Tara had annoyed her.

"Oh, go on then," she agreed, taking the paper and signing her name with a flourish. She tossed the paper over to her sister and signed the other one.

Pop Diva

Lolly looked at the paper where it lay. "I really don't think…" She hesitated.

"Oh, don't be mean," said Pop. "Go on. Do it just this once. We've never been asked for our autographs at school before!" Pop couldn't help feeling flattered by the girls' attention. She looked at her sister and grinned. "You'd better get used to it," she told her. "Once we're number one in the download charts and have made a pop video, *everyone* in the whole, wide world will recognize us!"

3 Pop's Plans

After tea, the girls went back to their room and Pop finished unpacking.

"Wow. That's a nice camera," said Chloe to Lolly, who had just put a shiny new digital camera on her bed.

"We both had cameras for Christmas," Lolly explained. "I wanted one to help with biology and geography projects. But I'll take some pictures of us all as well. I can print them out from my laptop. It'll be fun."

"Cool!" said Chloe. "Thanks."

"And this is my camera," announced Pop, pulling a slightly larger case out of her trunk. "I got one that takes digital movies. I got a tripod for it as well," she added, diving into her case again and revealing the tripod, which she unfolded and set up at the end of her bed. "As soon as I knew we'd got the record contract, I just had to have one. It'll help plan the dance moves to go with our songs."

"Oh," said Chloe.

Pop noticed her friend's puzzled expression. "We're bound to make videos to go with the songs we release," she explained. "And I thought it would be good fun to film myself trying out a few ideas. You can do all sorts of special effects with the software," she added.

"I thought you just wanted to be a model, a pop singer and a TV presenter. Now you're planning on being choreographer, cameraman and video producer as well," observed Tara sarcastically. "Is there no end to your talents?"

Pop had the grace to blush. "Someone else would film the video, *obviously*," she said. "The camera is just to help me work out some ideas."

"The main thing will be getting the song right in the studio," Lolly added quietly.

Pop smiled at her sister. "Of *course* it will," she agreed. The very thought of making their first single made a huge bubble of excitement burst out of her. She grabbed Chloe and whirled her around the room, narrowly missing the tripod.

"You're so lucky," panted Chloe when they came to a stop.

"But it'll be you next," enthused Pop, "and then Tara and then we'll *all* be mega music stars together. How about that? Maybe you could both be in our first video. Pop 'n' Lolly 'n' friends!" Then another thought hit her.

"We could *all* practise being stars with my camera," she said slowly. "After all, we do need to know how we look on TV, so that we can be at our best when our big breaks happen."

Tara shook her head. "I don't care what I look like when I play bass," she growled. "It's the music that's important."

"Maybe if you're in a *band*," acknowledged Pop grudgingly. "Though I'm sure loads of rock musicians spend ages on their look. Anyway, we're pop singers – Chloe, Lolly and me. Presentation counts for a lot. It's no good having a mega hit if you look dreadful. With us, it's the whole package that counts."

The more she thought about it, the more Pop was certain she was on to something. "We ought to be having *lessons* on TV interview techniques," she told the others. "The school ought to be teaching us how to act."

"I think it does do a bit of that later on for the older students," said Lolly, but Pop wasn't listening.

"It doesn't matter," she carried on. "Because we can do it ourselves, now. We can practise what to say about our latest hit in front of my camera."

"But you don't even know what this amazing hit is actually going to *be* yet," said Tara.

Pop looked a bit abashed. "True. They haven't decided yet. The record company is going to send several songs to Mr. Player, so we can rehearse them before going to the studio."

She smiled at Chloe. "You don't know when you'll

get a recording contract, Chloe. But it doesn't matter, does it? You can still practise your TV technique."

"I suppose..." said Chloe uncertainly.

"And I don't mind interviewing you," Pop offered. A sudden thought hit her and she beamed widely. "I'll do the interviews. It will be good preparation for when I'm presenting my own TV show!"

Tara groaned theatrically.

"It *will*, Tara!" Pop insisted, high on excitement again. "We can have it all! Modelling, TV presenting and mega pop stardom, too. I'll help everyone get some interview practice. How about that? Come on, Chloe. Sit here and I'll interview you."

Chloe laughed. "I've got nothing interesting to say," she protested.

Pop looked at her with a serious expression on her face. "*Everyone* is interesting in their own way," she told Chloe. "It just needs a sympathetic person to bring it out."

Pop certainly *did* seem to be able to draw Chloe out. Even Tara stopped what she was doing and listened as

Pop Diva

Pop got Chloe to talk about her family and funny things that happened at home. When Pop played the piece back, Chloe put her hands up to her face in embarrassment.

"I wasn't going to say half of that!" she protested. "How did you wheedle it out of me? I sound so stupid."

"No, you don't," said Tara. "It was good hearing your family stories."

Everyone stared at Tara. It was very unlike her to praise anything. She looked cross and glared back at them. "Well," she snapped. "Credit where it's due."

"That's right," agreed Lolly. "It was a good interview, Pop. Chloe came across exactly as she really is."

"Good," said Pop, feeling very pleased. She was still fiddling about with her camera when Mrs. Pinto came to tell them it was time for lights out.

"That's a nice camera," she said, spotting Pop's present. "Did you get it for Christmas?"

When Pop told Mrs. Pinto about her plan to offer interview practice to her friends, the housemistress looked worried. "Don't go annoying people by insisting on interviewing them," she warned Pop. "I know you can get carried away with new ideas."

"Don't worry," Pop said. "I'll be sensible. After all, TV presenting is another career idea for me. It's not just messing about. I might become a chat-show host."

"Do you really *need* another career?" asked Mrs. Pinto. "After all, most people are happy with one and you have *two* so far!"

"But this is the first idea I've had about what to do if Lolly ends up studying medicine later on," Pop explained. "The other things – modelling and singing – are what we do together as twins. I need something that I can do on my own as well. I'm pretty sure my voice isn't strong enough for me to be a solo singer like Chloe, but I'd love to be a TV presenter!"

"Well, full marks for thinking ahead." Mrs. Pinto laughed. "But put the camera away for now, Pop. You all need your sleep. The first day of lessons is always tiring and you need to be at your best."

The housemistress switched off the light and closed

the door. As soon as she'd gone, Pop sat up and reached for the camera again. "Look at this!" she whispered. She switched on the camera and played back the last bit of film she'd taken.

"It's Mrs. Pinto!" Chloe giggled.

"I didn't realize you had the camera on!" said Lolly, watching the tiny screen. Mrs. Pinto's laugh came out of the camera and the girls all laughed too.

"So much for asking people's permission before you film them," said Tara.

"But Mrs. Pinto didn't say that I had to do that," Pop objected. "She only said that I shouldn't annoy them. And Mrs. Pinto wasn't annoyed."

"Pop, you're terrible!" said Lolly with a laugh. "How did I get lumbered with a sister like you?"

"I don't know," replied Pop, pointing the camera at Lolly. "Why do you think we *are* so different?"

Lolly slid down and hid under her duvet. "Don't film me in *bed*!" she protested in a muffled voice. "Go to sleep. We've got a singing lesson first thing in the morning!"

Pop turned the camera on herself and stared seriously into it. "This is Pop Lowther, model, pop star and TV presenter signing off," she said. "Goodnight."

4 Lesson Time

Because Pop and Lolly always sang as a duo, they had their singing lessons together. The first session of the new term was straight after breakfast and they had to eat quickly to get to Mr. Player's room in time. When they arrived, he was talking to Mrs. Jones, who played piano for him sometimes. Both gave the twins welcoming smiles.

"I hear that it's all good news for you just now," Mr. Player greeted them. "I know your agent has been hoping for a contract for some time and now you have one!"

"Yes!" agreed Pop enthusiastically. "Satin is really pleased. She told us that it would be a good idea to come to Rockley Park and she was right!"

"We still have to sing well enough to make a good single," Lolly said quietly.

Mr. Player looked at her approvingly. "You're right," he agreed. "And it will take a bit of work. I've had a letter from your record company telling me what they want you to learn. There are four songs. One has been written especially for you."

"Wow!" said Pop. "That sounds pretty cool."

"It's quite a tricky tune, but I think you should manage it okay," said Mr. Player. "Luckily, I know Gavin Randel, who will be your producer at the recording studio."

"Will that help?" asked Pop.

"Well, I've worked with him in the past and I know what sort of sound he likes," Mr. Player told them. "We've spoken on the phone about you and discussed what you're capable of."

"That's good!" said Lolly, looking relieved.

"He won't be expecting anything too clever, but that doesn't mean it will be easy," he added. "Every song must be spot on. Don't worry," he reassured Lolly, who was looking nervous again. "It'll be fine as long as you put plenty of effort in. And I'm sure you will."

"Of course!" said Pop airily. "Don't we always?"

"Come on, then," Mr. Player said. "Let's make a start. Could you play us some scales, please, Mrs. Jones? We'll start with a gentle warm-up and see how your voices are after all that Christmas pudding."

There wasn't time to try all the songs in depth, but they ran through them once or twice and discussed what they liked and disliked about each one.

"The lyrics are really silly in that one," said Pop, pointing to the title of the first song they'd tried.

"I know what you mean." Mr. Player laughed. "But the tune is good, don't you think? And it's actually quite challenging. You'll have a bit of work to do if you're really to get to grips with it."

Lolly nodded. "You're right," she agreed. "And I don't mind too much about the lyrics," she added. "It's really cool having a song written for us, even one called *Lollipop Lullaby*!"

Pop wrinkled her nose. "I prefer *Last Summer*," she said. "It's got a catchy tune and the words are really good. I hope we can release that one as a single."

Mr. Player looked at his watch. "That's it for now," he told them. "Practise over the next couple of days and we'll work hard on the songs next time. It shouldn't take you too long to learn how to sing them really well."

As soon as the singing lesson was over, the twins rushed to their English class. After that, it was the mid-morning break. Pop felt like some fun after all the hard work, and dug her camera out of her bag.

"Would you like me to interview you?" she asked Marmalade, who was deep in conversation with Danny outside the main school building.

Marmalade grinned. "You can interview me *any* time," he said. "What's it for?"

"So you can practise your TV technique for when you're famous," Pop told him. "And I can try out my interviewing technique at the same time."

Marmalade looked disappointed. "Oh," he said. "I thought you were interested in *me*."

"I am!" Pop told him, turning on the charm. "You're such a good dancer, and I know you've had problems with injury. You'll be a great person to interview when I'm a TV presenter with my own show."

Marmalade laughed. "Oh, go on then. I suppose it might help if someone wants to interview me for real one day!"

"Sit on the wall," Pop said. "Lolly will hold the camera, won't you, Lolly?"

Lolly sighed. "Okay," she agreed. "But it's freezing out here. Don't take too long. I was going to go to the loo, and it's biology next. I don't want to be late."

"I'll do the camera work if you like," offered Danny.

"Are you sure?" Lolly looked pleased. "It would be great if you could. I'll do it next time for you, Pop."

"Okay," Pop agreed. "Thanks. I'll just show you what to do, Danny."

By the time Pop, Danny and Marmalade had finished having fun with the camera, they were rather late for biology. They slid guiltily into their places and Mrs. Pinto gave them a hard look.

"I hope this isn't going to become a habit," she said. "We have a lot of work to get through this term."

Pop waited until the teacher had looked away and then she wrinkled her nose at Marmalade. He rolled his eyes in reply and she had to choke back a giggle. She didn't want to get told off again.

As the day wore on, Pop had a great time chatting to people on camera. Most of them were rather flattered to be asked, even when they realized that it wasn't for anything important. At teatime, Pop sat down to her chicken korma feeling very pleased with herself.

"How about you?" she asked Tara. "I don't have you on film yet." Pop didn't think Tara would be very easy to interview, but by now she was feeling really confident and was up for a challenge.

"Why would I want you to interview me?" Tara asked. "What's in it for me?"

"Well." Pop struggled to find a convincing reply. "It could help you in the future…"

"Yes, I've heard all that," Tara cut her off. "I tell you

what. Why don't I interview *you*?"

"Really?" That sounded like a great idea to Pop. She was always ready to talk about herself.

"Go on," urged Marmalade. "Let's see what *you're* like in the hot seat!"

"Yes," agreed Chloe. "Go for it, Pop."

"Fair enough," said Pop. "*I'll* show you all how it's done." Pop suspected that Tara might try to give her a hard time, but she was sure she could handle even the most awkward interviewer.

Tara took the camera and gave it to Lolly. "You know how to use it, don't you?" she asked.

"Yes," said Lolly. "Are you sure you want to do this?" she added to her sister.

"It's all right," said Pop confidently. "I'll never hear the last of it if I don't go through with it now."

Tara was busy scribbling down a few notes. "My guest today," she said into the camera, "is one half of the famous duo Pop and Lolly Lowther."

Pop smiled as Lolly turned the camera on her. "Hello," she said.

"Is it true that you're the noisiest of the two?" Tara asked provokingly.

Pop looked a bit disgruntled, then decided to treat the interview less seriously. After all, it was just a bit of fun. "Oh, yes!" she said. "My sister is quite serious and sensible. I'm the fun-loving one!"

"So was it down to *you*, getting the record deal?" asked Tara.

"Not at all," replied Pop truthfully. "Our agent got the contract. But it's a great chance for us, and we're going to give it all we've got."

"You're making a single, I hear."

Pop nodded.

"Are you going to be covering an old hit, or singing a new song?"

"Actually," said Pop proudly, "we have to learn four songs and the single hasn't been chosen yet. But one song *has* been specially written for us."

"Wow!" said Tara, sounding impressed in spite of herself. "I expect they'll want to use that, then. What's it called?"

"Um…" Pop hesitated. She had been excited when she'd heard that a song had been written for them, but it was the one with the lyrics she didn't like. It was probably going to be very commercial, but it was the cheesiest song she'd heard in a long time.

"Can't you remember?" asked Tara unkindly.

"Of course I can!" Pop replied crossly. "It's called *Lollipop Lullaby*."

A smile crept across Tara's usually grumpy face at this mumbled reply. "Would you like to repeat the title in case we didn't quite get it?" she teased.

"*Lollipop Lullaby*," Pop said again. She glared at Tara defiantly.

"Would you say it was a serious song?" Tara enquired.

"I get it," butted in Marmalade. "Lolly-Pop lullaby. What a laugh! Can you sing it with a straight face, Pop? How does it go?"

Lolly stopped filming her sister and laughed. "It *is* silly, isn't it?" she agreed. "But we're not allowed to make the decisions. I bet Tara is right and they choose to release that one."

"Go on then, Pop. Tell us what the lyrics are," begged Marmalade. "Give us all a laugh!"

"No!" said Pop furiously. "It's not a joke. Satin said it could be a big hit if we're lucky."

"And if we're *un*lucky," added Tara wickedly, "it could be an even bigger one!"

5 Teasing Pop

Pop spent the rest of the day being cross with both Tara and Marmalade.

"Take no notice," Lolly told her. "They'll soon stop if you don't let their comments get to you."

But Pop simply couldn't ignore the teasing. She had always wanted to be taken seriously as a singer, so her friends' jokes really annoyed her. When the evening's activities were over and it was time to go back to their houses for the night, Marmalade teased her one final time.

"'Night, girls," he called, setting off for the boys' house with Danny and Ed. "Don't forget to sing everyone your *Lollipop Lullaby* to get them to sleep, will you!" He mimed licking an imaginary lolly, then snored loudly.

Lolly laughed, but Pop was furious. "You're encouraging him!" she told her sister angrily. "And he's being really stupid."

"I don't know why you're so upset about it," Lolly said quietly. "I'm not. And I expect I'll feel just as silly as you when it comes to singing those words."

"*I* won't feel silly!" snapped Pop. "We're professionals, aren't we? The record company thinks it's the sort of thing that will sell for us, so we'd be silly to record anything else!"

"Most of the students would be thrilled to be making a single," added Chloe. "It doesn't matter what it's called."

But it *did* matter to Pop. She had never been very good at laughing at herself and she certainly didn't appreciate being teased.

Pop hoped that everyone would have forgotten about the song by the next day, but at lunchtime Marmalade entertained his companions by quoting the lyrics to them.

"Where did you get our lyrics from?" Pop demanded. She knew that neither she nor Lolly had left the words to the song lying about.

"A little bird gave them to me," replied Marmalade.

Pop flushed angrily. "You read them in Mr. Player's room!" she accused him. "I wondered why you were taking so long to leave after his last lesson. You must have been waiting until Lolly and I had left. How sneaky!"

"There aren't any rules about not reading other students' lyrics," Marmalade reminded her reasonably.

It was true. And even Marmalade, whose main subject was dance, had singing lessons with the rest of his class. There was no reason why he shouldn't have a look through all the music lying around. Mr. Player had a habit of making sure the students' music was easily accessible, in case they needed it. It wouldn't have taken Marmalade more than a minute or two to locate the twins' song and read the lyrics. Unfortunately for Pop, Marmalade had a very good memory. He had learned almost the whole song just so that he could tease her!

Maybe Lollipop Lullaby *is a bit cheesy,* she thought. *But Tara and Marmalade won't feel like laughing if it really does become a big hit.*

Pop didn't want to let their teasing take the shine off her recording contract, but she was very annoyed with her friends. *How dare they laugh at me?* she fumed. *I'll show them. I'll think of something else to do to prove just how multi-talented I really am!*

She thought about the TV interview that had happened over Christmas. If only Pop could land a presenter's job! But she knew that there was no real chance of that at the moment. Then she remembered the school concert. Okay, so it wasn't TV, but someone had to present it. That someone was usually a member of staff, but surely there was no reason why it shouldn't be a student? And it would show Marmalade and Tara that she could handle much more than a song with silly lyrics. She was also someone to be depended on and taken seriously.

"Dreaming about your number one?" asked Chloe, as Pop sat deep in thought.

"You never know," Pop said to her. "Stranger things have happened, haven't they? Wouldn't it be wonderful?"

"She's planning the album now," said Tara with a smirk. "I expect it'll be called *Lollipop La La*."

"Actually, I was planning when to go and see the Principal," Pop told them. She smiled when she saw their surprised faces. Even Lolly didn't know what Pop was up to.

Pop had resolved to go and see Mrs. Sharkey as soon as she could. The next concert would be at half-term, as usual, so there was no time to lose to put her new idea into action.

"What are you going to see the Principal for?" asked Marmalade curiously.

"Aha!" said Pop. "Wouldn't you like to know? Come on, Lolly. Hurry up or we'll be late for our lesson."

Their next lesson was singing with Mr. Player and the girls were due to work on *Lollipop Lullaby*.

"Honestly, Pop, you should know the words by

now," said Mr. Player as she stumbled over the chorus. "I know you've only had them a couple of days, but usually you're so quick to memorize lyrics. It's: *With lots of Lolly and lots of Pop, it's a lollipop lullaby.*"

"Sorry," apologized Pop.

"Let's try it again. I want you to concentrate on the phrasing. Breathe here," he told Pop, pointing at the lyrics. "You shouldn't try and sing the whole line with one breath. It sounds too forced."

"You won't get distracted from our songs, will you?" said Lolly anxiously after the lesson. Pop had told her sister about her idea of presenting the concert and Lolly was getting rather concerned. "I'm worried that you're taking on too much."

Pop gave Lolly a quick hug. "Don't worry," she told her. "I can handle it."

With the day packed full of lessons, Pop wasn't able to see Mrs. Sharkey until just after tea. But as soon as she could, she nipped up the stairs to the Principal's room and knocked on the open door.

"Hello, Pop," said Mrs. Sharkey from behind her

huge desk. "What can I do for you? I hear things are going well at the moment career-wise. You must be thrilled at your record deal."

"Yes, thank you," replied Pop. It was always a bit scary speaking to Mrs. Sharkey, even when you weren't in trouble, so she drew herself up to her full height and tried to sound confident. "I wanted to speak to you about the next concert," she said.

"Oh?"

Pop outlined her idea and Mrs. Sharkey listened carefully.

"Well, I do think it's a good idea to let students have a go at presenting concerts," said Mrs. Sharkey once Pop had finished. "We could have several presenters for each concert or just one. Maybe we should ask for volunteers." She looked at Pop. "Or did you think you could do it all?"

Pop blushed. "Well..." she began.

Mrs. Sharkey gave her a knowing smile. "You'd like to do it all yourself," she finished for her student. Pop nodded and Mrs. Sharkey laughed. "I thought as much," the Principal said. "Don't worry. You'd never make it in the entertainment world if you were a shrinking violet, but you know that already, don't you?"

"Yes," agreed Pop eagerly.

"Well, I'm not so sure about you doing it all, but as you thought of the idea, I don't see any problem in you having the first shot at it," said Mrs. Sharkey. "I'll have a word with the staff and see how they'd like to handle it. Judge Jim isn't back from sick leave yet, but when he is I expect he'll be very enthusiastic. He likes it when the students show a bit of initiative."

"Thank you!" said Pop, really excited that Mrs. Sharkey had agreed to her idea so easily.

"You'll have to make certain that it doesn't interfere with any of your other work though," Mrs. Sharkey warned. "I'm sure you'll keep focused on the singing, but your other lessons are important too."

Pop nodded hastily. Mrs. Sharkey always said this to her students.

As she left and closed the door behind her, Pop let a big smile fill her face. Wait until Tara and Marmalade heard what she was going to be doing at the concert as well as singing with Lolly. Maybe she'd even get an extra Rising Stars point for being a brilliant presenter! Pop and Lolly hadn't won enough points to appear in the Rising Stars Concert last term, so perhaps this would help to boost their total for the next one.

She raced down the stairs and over to the girls' boarding house. It would soon be homework time, but for now her three roommates were all together in their bedroom.

"Guess what!" Pop announced, bursting in excitedly.

Lolly looked up from the book she was reading and smiled at her excited sister. "So it was a 'yes', then?" she enquired.

Pop nodded, her eyes shining.

"What was a yes?" asked Chloe.

Tara didn't say anything, but Pop could see that she had stopped what she was doing and was waiting for the reply.

"I'm going to be an official presenter of the half-term concert," Pop announced. "It's all arranged. Mrs.

Sharkey thinks it's a great idea and of course it'll be excellent practice for my eventual TV career!"

"Wow!" said Chloe. "Whose idea was that?"

"Mine," Pop admitted, feeling very pleased with herself.

"Typical!" snorted Tara. "Trust you to hog the limelight."

"It's no good being a shrinking violet in this business," Pop told her primly. "Besides," she added, "you'll get your chance, Tara. Mrs. Sharkey is thinking of asking for volunteers in future. I'm only doing it this time because it was my idea."

"That's fair enough," agreed Chloe.

"And it's a *good* idea," added Tara, to Pop's surprise. "Well, it *is*," she repeated. "Being a presenter is another way of interacting with the audience, while keeping control. We all need to be good at that."

Pop stared at Tara. It hadn't occurred to her how useful the skill would be to them all as performers.

"Thank you, Tara," she said with a grin, the teasing all forgiven. "I'm glad you can see there's more to me than *Lollipop Lullaby*!"

6 A Bit of a Hitch

There certainly *was* more to both Pop and Lolly than *Lollipop Lullaby*, but the song promised to be the highlight of their careers so far. Pop loved revelling in the excitement of knowing that she and Lolly were proper members of the pop world. Their record deal proved it!

But while Lolly continued to concentrate on learning the songs as well as doing her schoolwork, Pop was more interested in enjoying feeling like a real pop star. And that didn't seem to include working hard towards being one. She had always been a true professional, but she now felt as if the single was a done deal and didn't need too much input from her. She had always had a butterfly mind and found it difficult to concentrate on her academic work, even though she knew it was important. Now she was riding so high on a tide of anticipated success that she felt able to turn her hand to anything. A modelling career had been theirs for years, now a record deal was in the bag and she was determined to become a TV presenter as well. Why not? Pop was sure she could handle it all.

But all was not well. Pop might have been breezing her way from day to fun-filled day, but Mr. Player was becoming exasperated with her. He was a professional too, and knew the music industry inside out, having once been a famous singer himself. He could see the value of kooky, off-the-wall songs. Any of the tracks they were learning could well be a real success for the twins, but whichever song was chosen, it had to be executed perfectly. No record company would spend money promoting a single that was badly put together and the girls had to prove they could do it.

"Come on, Pop. You're not concentrating," he said for the umpteenth time during an early morning lesson.

"The record company won't be very pleased with you if you can't sound better than that! You were singing flat just then!"

"Sorry." Pop dragged her mind back from where she'd been planning what to say at the beginning of the concert. Something aspirational was needed to get everyone in the mood. "Shall we do it again?" she offered.

"No," said Mr. Player. "We've run out of time now. I want you to practise with Lolly before the next lesson, though. It's not as if you can't do it. But you're not putting in anything like enough effort. And your solo part in *Lollipop Lullaby* needs a lot of work."

Once outside Mr. Player's room, Pop shrugged off his comments. "We're not scheduled to go into the recording studio until next week," she told her sister. "I'll have a go at it over the weekend. It'll be fine then. Guess what!" she added. "I've been thinking about how to welcome all the parents and everybody to the concert. It should be quite a speech."

Lolly stared at her sister. "What do you mean – a

speech?" she asked. "I thought you were introducing the acts, not giving a speech!"

"Well..." Pop blushed. "Perhaps it won't exactly be a *speech*, but I do have to work out how to welcome everyone."

"Pop! I think you're getting a bit carried away with this," said Lolly in a shocked voice. "You know Mrs. Sharkey always does that part of the concert."

Pop shrugged. "But she might suggest I do it," she told Lolly. "So I need to be prepared, just in case."

"You ought to be spending more time on things you *know* you have to do, not making up speeches you might never need," said Lolly, sounding really worried.

Pop scowled. "I'm ambitious," she said. "And if that means working on something I might not use, then so be it." The way she put it made it sound as if Pop was being virtuous, but she could see that her sister wasn't convinced. "If you don't like it, you can lump it," she added stubbornly. She broke into a run and headed back to the house, leaving Lolly speechless.

Pushing her sister's warning to the back of her mind,

Pop Diva

Pop concentrated on her preparations for the half-term concert. With over a week until the recording was scheduled, there was plenty of time to get her solo sorted out. Meanwhile, she was having fun planning her role in the concert. Could she think of a brilliant idea to put her stamp on it? She thought hard and eventually an idea popped into her head. How about if she recorded herself chatting to the performers and got the interviews flashed up on a big screen between each act? That would give the school concert a really different, classy look. And it would all be because of her! She ought to make a note to suggest this to Mrs. Sharkey.

As well as that Pop decided she would send some film of herself presenting the concert to the producer she'd met briefly when she and Lolly had been interviewed on TV. She knew he was also one of the producers of a pop programme that was often hosted by guest presenters. Yes! That would be a good way in, especially when *Lollipop Lullaby* started to do well. With her song rocketing up the charts, the producer would be *bound* to want Pop as a guest presenter. From there, it would only be a small step to maybe even having her own programme!

Of course, she'd send the same clips to their agent. Satin was bound to approve. Who knows *where* all this exposure would get her? Pop could be *mega* famous in no time!

When she got back to the house, Pop looked in her pigeonhole, as she usually did. Often it was empty, but sometimes her parents sent a card or letter giving them all the news from home. Today there was something, but it wasn't a letter. It was an internal note telling Pop to go and see Mrs. Sharkey.

Pop had got over her fear of seeing the Principal. In fact, she welcomed the opportunity. *I can tell her about my recorded interviews idea,* she told herself as she dumped her school books and picked up a notebook. She might need to jot down other things about the concert that Mrs. Sharkey wanted to discuss with her and she wanted to look efficient.

Pop met Lolly and Chloe coming into the house as

she was leaving it. She felt a twinge of guilt about telling her sister to lump it. After all, Lolly was only trying to help. But Pop didn't want to say anything in front of Chloe. She could apologize later if Lolly was still cross. Instead, she touched her sister's arm affectionately and flashed her a smile. "I have a meeting with Mrs. Sharkey," she told them both in an upbeat voice. "I'll see you later."

She skipped over to the main house and up the stairs. The secretary wasn't at her desk, but Mrs. Sharkey's door was open. When she saw Pop, Mrs. Sharkey beckoned her in.

"You wanted to see me?" said Pop, suddenly feeling rather less confident.

The Principal's expression wasn't very encouraging.

"I get very tired of warning students that their schoolwork mustn't suffer when they want to take on extra things," she told Pop. "I expect you all get tired of hearing me say it too."

Pop wasn't sure if she was supposed to reply, so she said nothing.

"But I always mean what I say," continued Mrs. Sharkey. "And there are no exceptions to the rule. It doesn't matter how famous you are. Students who can't keep up with their academic and musical lessons don't get to do extra things. Now, I have your projected grades here."

"Oh," said Pop.

"Yes. Oh," agreed Mrs. Sharkey grimly. "Not only are all the academic staff grumbling about you, but Mr. Player is displeased as well. I *am* surprised at that. You're usually so professional at anything to do with your career. Now, more than ever, you need to be properly prepared. When is your recording scheduled for?"

"Not until next week," said Pop.

"Well, in Mr. Player's opinion, you aren't anything like ready for a recording session yet," the Principal told her. "So, you'd better find time for plenty of extra rehearsals to make sure that you *are* completely ready in time." Mrs. Sharkey looked sharply at Pop. "If you perform badly, it will reflect on the school," she said.

Pop Diva

"And then I'll be *really* angry with you. So there'll be no more talk of you presenting the concert until your work improves. All of it. And I don't want to hear any protests," she added, as Pop started to speak. "I want to see that your actual grades are a lot better than these projections. If they are satisfactory, you can go ahead, but *not* unless they are."

Pop went back downstairs in a very bad mood. *It's not fair,* she told herself. *I'm never going to be very good at stuff like maths and science, so why should I be made to study them?* But in her heart she knew there was no getting away from Mrs. Sharkey's ultimatum. If she wanted to present the concert at half-term, she'd simply have to knuckle down and make more of an effort.

At least I don't have to tell anyone what she said, Pop told herself. *If I keep it to myself and get reasonable grades, I'll still be the concert presenter and no one will be any the wiser.*

As she made her way back to the girls' house, she tried to think of a convincing reason to tell the others for having been to see the Principal. But when she arrived back in her room, all thoughts of making up stories were forgotten when she saw her sister's face.

"Whatever's the matter?" she asked Lolly. Her sister was looking pale and worried. Pop's heart turned over. "Are you all right? Has there been an accident?" she asked. "Tell me! What's happened?"

"Satin just phoned," said Lolly. "The record company has been in touch with her to say that one of their stars is ill and can't work tomorrow. They've got an expensive London studio booked and don't want to waste the booking."

"So?" asked Pop in bewilderment.

"They asked Satin if we'd step in to do our recording tomorrow, instead of next week," Lolly added. She looked anxiously at her sister to gauge her reaction.

The world seemed to stop for Pop as the enormity of the situation hit her. Her hands flew up to her face and her heart almost stopped beating. Make the recording tomorrow? She hadn't planned on that! Surely they couldn't make her do it *tomorrow*? "What did Satin say?" she asked weakly, but she could see the answer in Lolly's face.

"She said yes," Lolly told her. "She said that we were always on top of things and she was sure it would be all right."

Pop groaned. She had been confident about being ready in a week, but not by tomorrow. She wasn't good enough, and she knew it.

7 A Good Idea

Pop knew that Chloe and Tara must be watching to see her reaction, but she was so appalled at the news that she didn't care. Instead of putting on a brave face, she sank down on her bed. "*Why* did Satin agree?" she demanded. "She should have rung Mr. Player first to find out if we were ready. And she shouldn't change our schedule unless she asks us first!"

"She said that the producer will understand if we need a little bit of rehearsal time to make sure the track is spot on," said Lolly, not pointing out that it was only Pop who wasn't prepared. "It's only a few days earlier than we expected."

"A few days can make all the difference," moaned

Pop Diva

Pop. "I can't record tomorrow. It's impossible. Whatever are we going to do?" She took a deep breath and tried to concentrate. *There must be a way out*, she told herself. *I just need a bit more time.* "I know," she said, brightening up slightly. "I'll phone and tell Satin we can't do it. They'll have to find someone else to fill their empty slot. It's not *our* fault some singer is ill!" That seemed a very good idea. Why should she and Lolly be the ones to have to change their plans?

Pop rummaged in her bag and brought out her mobile. She saw Chloe and Tara exchanging glances, but she ignored them. They didn't have agents, so they couldn't possibly understand. After all, wasn't Satin supposed to make sure the timing was right before she signed them up to anything?

"Pop?" It was Lolly, still looking worried.

"What?"

"Do you think you ought to?"

Pop gave her sister a withering look and opened her phone. She got through to Satin straight away, but the twins' agent wasn't in the mood for excuses.

A Good Idea

"You knew you had this recording coming up," she told Pop. "And I know Rockley Park prepares its students very well for any engagement. What's the problem? You can't tell me you're not ready."

That was exactly what Pop wanted to say, but she was far too ashamed to admit it. "The thing is, I've been busy doing other things," she tried to explain.

"Like what?" demanded Satin. "You don't do modelling assignments during term time."

"No…well…you know how it is," said Pop feebly. Somehow, it didn't seem the right time to tell Satin about her concert-presenting plans. Pop could tell that she was only interested in current work, not future ideas.

"Listen, Poppy," said Satin seriously. "I've worked hard to get you this recording contract. You've got it on the back of your success as models and the professionalism you show in that world. I assured the company that you are totally reliable and are always well prepared. You're very young and you have an awful lot to prove."

Pop Diva

"I know that," said Pop, but Satin wasn't listening.

"If you can show that you're mature enough to be able to help out, you're likely to get more work," Satin continued. "Studio time is very expensive and record companies don't want to waste it. If you're really not ready, you must say so. But if you're telling me that you can't sing tomorrow, then goodness knows what will happen." Satin sounded really harassed. "You may find that *your* scheduled day is cancelled and given to the artist who had to pull out of tomorrow's session," she told Pop. "He's a big money-earner for the company and has a deadline for his album recordings, while at the moment you're not important at all." Satin paused.

Pop adjusted the phone in her hand and turned away from Tara and Chloe so they couldn't see her horrified expression.

"I don't think you really understand the significance of all this," Satin went on. "It might be okay, but on the other hand, your recording could be postponed for *months*. They think the timing is good right now to release a song like yours, but who knows what the climate might be like later on in the year? Are you prepared to lose this opportunity? And, don't forget, you're under contract to this company. If they choose to ignore you for a while, you can't just go and sign with someone else."

"Oh," said Pop, her heart sinking even further. "I didn't realize it was like that."

"It's unfortunate," agreed Satin. "But this is big business and the record companies have to make tough decisions. What could be a big break for you is just a way of making a profit for the company."

"I see," said Pop dismally. "Okay."

There was no way she could pull out. If she did, it could ruin their careers. And maybe it wouldn't be so bad. She was okay with most of the songs. It was only the solo on *Lollipop Lullaby* that she was shaky on. Even so, she put her phone back into her pocket with a terrible sense of foreboding. She took a deep breath and gave Lolly a brittle smile. "Well!" she said. "It looks like we're going to be in the recording studio tomorrow. Shall we go and have a practice?"

Pop Diva

Pop took every chance she could to practise during the rest of the day, but it wasn't easy. There was a full afternoon of lessons to get through and the twins weren't scheduled another singing lesson that day.

"Let's go and see Mr. Player," urged Lolly during the afternoon break. "I'm sure he'll arrange for us to miss English and geography so we can practise properly, when he knows we're going to be recording tomorrow."

That was undoubtedly true, but Pop knew he would also be very angry with her for not working on the song properly when she had the chance. The other teachers would be cross too and might complain again to Mrs. Sharkey. Pop knew that she *ought* to ask for her singing teacher's help, but she just couldn't bring herself to risk another telling-off from him and the Principal.

The girls managed to squeeze in a bit of practice after tea, and after homework time Pop suggested a last effort before bed.

"I can't," said Lolly. "I need to rest my voice, Pop.

A Good Idea

Otherwise, I'm not going to be any good in the morning. I think I might have a cold coming."

"Great!" said Pop dismally. "That's all we need. Well, I'll run through the songs one more time on my own. I expect that'll do."

But Pop was still having difficulty with her solo for *Lollipop Lullaby*. Even now it just wasn't right. Because her phrasing was out, she couldn't control her breathing properly and she badly needed Mr. Player's coaching to overcome the problem. Well, it was too late now. She would just have to do the best she could and hope that her best was good enough.

8 A Recording Nightmare

After an early breakfast, Pop and Lolly were whisked off to London in the car that had been sent for them. If Pop had been feeling more confident, she would have enjoyed the journey, but she was too concerned about what was to come. She and Lolly knew very well that hoping for the best wasn't a very good way of approaching a professional engagement.

Because the session was at such short notice, the twins' mum couldn't arrange to be with them. Pop longed for her mum to be there to give her a hug, but instead the school sent along a member of the office staff as a chaperone. It was all right for Lolly. She had been sensible and would be fine, but Pop had never felt so scared and lonely before. And it didn't help that she knew it was all her own fault.

Once they were at the recording studio, the atmosphere couldn't help but impress them. It was one of the most well known studios in London, and not many people got to see it from the inside. It was very quiet, and there were no echoes in the carpeted reception area. It made them almost want to whisper.

The girl on the reception desk rang for someone to meet them. While their chaperone sat reading a music magazine, Pop and Lolly wandered up and down a long corridor, where there were lots of signed glossy photographs on the walls. The twins looked at them all. Some names and faces were very famous indeed.

"I wonder if our picture will be up there one day?" mused Lolly quietly. "I can't believe we're here, can you? It's a bit different from the studio at school, isn't it?" She linked arms with her sister and gave her a reassuring squeeze. Lolly cared about how her sister felt, and was doing her best to cheer Pop up, but nothing she said made Pop feel the least bit better.

Pop Diva

Soon Simon, the assistant engineer, arrived to take them to the studio where they would be working. "There are three studios in this building," he told them. "We can record a full orchestra in here," he said proudly, as he gave them a swift guided tour of the building. "There aren't many recording studios big enough to do that! We're setting up the chairs, music stands and microphones today, ready for a recording tomorrow."

Pop and Lolly peered into the room. It was a vast space with a special wall covering to absorb as much sound as possible. "We only want to record the sounds the instruments are making," he explained when he saw their interest, "not echoes off the walls."

They watched all the activity for a couple of minutes. Several people were setting out rows of chairs, while someone else was fixing microphones onto stands. There were miles of thin, black cables snaking everywhere.

"Why is that person chalking marks on a chair?" asked Pop, wondering if it was for a special member of the orchestra.

A Recording Nightmare

Simon laughed. "It's no good if the chairs squeak while the musicians are sitting on them during a recording," he told her. "Mark has just found a noisy one and is marking it to be got rid of. We're always having to buy new chairs!"

He led them on to one of the two smaller recording studios. Although the smallest of the three, it was still much bigger than Mr. Timms's recording studio at school, and the mixing desk was enormous!

In the control room, Simon introduced them to the sound engineer and then the producer, John Atlas. Pop and Lolly exchanged dismayed glances. Mr. Player had told them that Gavin Randel was going to be their producer, but this was a different person!

"I thought Gavin Randel was going to produce our songs," Pop said nervously.

"He's in charge overall," explained John, the producer they'd just been introduced to. "But he's not available today, so I'm going to get the tracks laid down and then he'll mix them next week. I see your record company has got *Lollipop Lullaby* marked as favourite for the first single, so let's see if we can give Gavin a really good recording to work with."

Pop's heart sank. John Atlas was obviously a no-nonsense kind of person. She couldn't imagine him being sympathetic or understanding. She had hoped Mr. Player's friend might have heard about her difficulties, and been able to help her out. But this man didn't know anything about Pop and Lolly. She had a nasty feeling that her best just wouldn't be good enough for him. And worse than that, the record company wanted to release the song she couldn't sing. Today was a disaster already.

"If you could go through to the recording booth, we'll have a run-through and get some levels set," the producer told them. "We need to make a start."

The producer was obviously very professional and wanted to get on with his job. He wasn't about to waste time mollycoddling badly prepared artists.

Pop and Lolly went into the recording booth and put on the headphones that were waiting for them. Suddenly, they could hear Simon's voice in their ears.

A Recording Nightmare

He was speaking into a small microphone in the control room, which fed into their headphones. "I'm going to play each tune for you, so you can run through them," he said. "I'll set the levels, and then when you're ready, give us the nod and we'll try a recording. Just relax and enjoy yourselves."

To begin with, all was well. The first three songs were fine. Pop wasn't at her sparkling best, but she knew the words and her phrasing was competent enough. Several times, the producer asked them to sing part of a song again, or suggested a change, but he seemed happy with their efforts overall. Then they had a break and a quick drink and it was time for *Lollipop Lullaby*. When Pop put her cup down she noticed that she was so nervous her hand was shaking.

To begin with, Lolly had to go into the recording booth to sing her part of the song. She only needed a few attempts before John Atlas was satisfied. Pop listened to her from the control room and was impressed. Lolly really was singing well. If only she could perform half as well as her sister, she'd be pleased.

When it came to Pop's turn, she went in with a heavy heart. She was sure she would be a disaster, and she was right.

Time after time, the producer halted the recording to get Pop to repeat a few notes, but it was hopeless. The more she was made to go over her part, the worse it got. In the end, she was so flustered that she was even forgetting some of the words.

"Is this the best you can manage?" John asked as Pop failed yet again to sing as well as she should have done.

"Sorry," she apologized into the microphone. She could see the producer muttering to the engineer through the glass partition that divided the recording booth from the control room, and she was sure he was being rude about her.

After yet another disastrous take, John Atlas beckoned Pop through into the control room. "Okay," he said. "You can have that chair." He pointed to a nearby swivel chair and Pop sat in it nervously, ready for a thorough telling-off. But it didn't come. In fact, the producer totally ignored her.

"Right," he said to Lolly. "Can you sing your sister's part? It's that solo line we really need."

"Er…I think so," said Lolly.

"Would you mind giving it a go?" he asked.

"All right," she agreed, looking at Pop. Pop gave her a thumbs-up. The producer must have decided to get Lolly to show Pop how it was done. He wasn't to know that they had practised together yesterday to no avail, but Pop was determined to watch and listen really hard and try to get it right next time.

"When you're ready," the producer told Lolly.

As soon as she nodded, the engineer ran the tape and the backing track played into Lolly's headphones. Pop could see her counting herself in. The producer nodded to the engineer as Lolly began to sing.

"Did you get that?" he asked the engineer, when Lolly had finished.

"Yep," said the engineer. "Would you like me to play it back?"

"Thanks."

Pop listened again as Lolly's taped version of Pop's part was played back.

"I think I see now…" Pop started, but the producer still took no notice of her.

"Can you sing it again from the second chorus?" he asked Lolly.

"Okay," Lolly agreed.

Pop was getting impatient. "I think I can do it now," she told the producer.

John Atlas glanced at her briefly. "You don't—" he began. "Hang on… Yes, sing from there to the end," he told Lolly as the tape ran. The backing track was rewound again and Lolly did as she was asked.

Pop got up from her chair and approached the mixing desk. "I'd like to try again now," she told them.

But the producer shook his head. "Let's just hear the last few bars," he said. The engineer played back Lolly's voice singing the last bit of Pop's part, including her solo, and everyone listened. "Thank you, Lolly. You can come through now," he said. Lolly came into the control room and John Atlas looked at his watch. "Thanks, girls," he said to them both. "I think we've got everything we need now. Just ask at reception for your car and they'll bring it round."

"But I need to record my solo!" protested Pop. "I haven't recorded every bit of my part yet! You must have forgotten."

"I haven't forgotten," John Atlas told Pop coldly. "Your sister did it instead. We don't have time to waste on children who can't be bothered to learn their song properly!"

9 Misery

Pop and Lolly hardly spoke on the way back to school. Pop's mood veered wildly between fury at the way she'd been treated and shame that she'd let herself and everyone else down so badly.

"It'll be all right," Lolly tried to tell her in a low voice so the chaperone wouldn't hear. "No one need know. They probably won't be able to tell from the single once it's been mixed anyway."

"But *I'll* know," protested Pop furiously. With every mile that went by, she felt worse and worse. How could she possibly have been so stupid? She'd allowed herself to get sidetracked with other things when she should have been concentrating on singing. TV work could be part of her future, but that single was *now*!

Pop decided that the first thing she must do when she got back was to put her camera away. She couldn't afford to waste any more time on it. She would tell Mrs. Sharkey that she wouldn't have time to present the concert, even if her grades *did* improve. Pop hated the idea of giving it up, but she knew she'd been wrong to take on the presenting when she should have been rehearsing her songs.

She sneaked a look at Lolly, who was looking out of the car window. Pop knew that she had no one to blame but herself for what had happened and yet poor Lolly was obviously feeling miserable as well. That was Pop's fault too. She took a deep breath. There wasn't much she could put right about this dreadful day, but there was one thing she *could* do. She put her hand on her sister's arm and squeezed it.

"Don't you worry, Lol," she said, trying to sound upbeat. "None of this is your fault. You did really well today."

"Thanks," said Lolly. "At least it's over now."

Pop Diva

But it wasn't over for Pop. When they got back to school they were just in time for a late tea and of course *everyone* wanted to know about their day.

"How'd you get on?" asked Chloe as soon as she saw them. "Was it exciting?"

"Sort of," replied Lolly.

"Exhausting," added Pop. "I think I might go back to our room, Lol. I've got a bit of a headache."

Pop couldn't bear to join in the chatter. And it would be much worse when the single came out without her voice on it. Everyone would be congratulating them and Pop would know that she didn't deserve any of the praise. She slunk out of the dining room and straight into the person she least wanted to see.

"Ah! Pop. There you are," said Mrs. Sharkey. "I think you'd better come up to my room."

The Principal led the way and Pop followed her dolefully up the stairs.

"I telephoned the recording studio this afternoon to find out how you'd got on," she told Pop. "It's not good news, is it?"

"No," agreed Pop. "I'm afraid not. But I've made a decision."

"Is it the sort of decision that might stop me writing a letter to your parents?" enquired Mrs. Sharkey coolly.

Pop gulped. A letter to her parents was the last thing she wanted. Pop felt tears pricking behind her eyes and she did her best to hold them back. "I know it was stupid not to be properly prepared in good time for the recording," she admitted to the Principal. "But I didn't realize we could be called in early. I thought it would be a good idea to have a TV career in the future and I just got carried away with thinking about that instead of working on the songs. I won't do the concert presenting now. Of course I won't." She glanced quickly at Mrs. Sharkey. "And I'm going to bury the camera at the bottom of my trunk and not take it out again *ever*."

"Well, I'm glad to see you're willing to admit your mistakes," said Mrs. Sharkey wryly. "But I'd rather you gave the camera to me for safe keeping until the end of term."

"All right," agreed Pop sadly.

"I have to say, I'm not very impressed with your agent either," Mrs. Sharkey continued. "There's been a bit of a breakdown in communication between her and the school. We act for most of our students, which means we know what's going on, but because you had an agent before you came to the school, things have been rather different. She really should have consulted Mr. Player before she agreed to an earlier date. I will have to write to her about it."

"None of this is Satin's fault!" said Pop quickly. "She told me I ought to pull out if I wasn't ready, but I thought I could do it and I didn't want to risk the recording being cancelled."

"Hmm," said the Principal. "You don't need to take *all* of the blame, Pop. You have been guilty of unprofessional behaviour, but Satin is supposed to look after your best interests and we are supposed to protect you as far as possible from bad experiences. I'm sorry. We *all* have lessons to learn." She paused. "I will be putting new measures in place to ensure that this doesn't happen again," she told Pop. "Agents like Satin *must* consult the school before agreeing to anything on the pupils' behalf. If Satin had only phoned me or Mr. Player, it would have been obvious that bringing the recording forward was most unwise, but the first I heard about it was when my secretary was arranging your chaperone. It's not good enough."

Pop began to feel a bit better, but Mrs. Sharkey hadn't finished. She fixed her steely eyes on Pop and Pop knew that she wasn't going to be let off that easily.

"However, none of this alters the fact that you are quite old enough to know how important it is to be well prepared in advance of any engagement," she went on angrily. "It's one of the first things we teach you here. You have no excuse for your unprofessional behaviour. This is your last chance, Poppy. Your grave lack of preparation has done us all a great disservice, especially Mr. Player. I will want to hear that you have apologized to him, and I want to see that camera of yours on my desk by this time tomorrow. And there'd better not be any more complaints about your schoolwork."

Pop Diva

"I know," said Pop. "And I really am sorry."

Pop went over to the girls' house feeling very shaken. She had always shrugged off complaints in the past, but what Mrs. Sharkey had said made her think hard for the first time in ages. The thing that hurt most was to be told that she had behaved in an unprofessional manner. Pop had always prided herself on her professionalism, but she knew that Mrs. Sharkey was right. For a start, Pop should have been ready when the studio call came and secondly, knowing how badly prepared she was, she should have had the courage to admit as much to Satin.

To her relief, the house was quiet. Pop made herself a cup of hot chocolate, took it along to her room, and sat on her bed. She realized that she had been living a charmed life for ages. She and Lolly did have the sort of life loads of girls would love, but while Lolly was a modest person and never overrated her abilities, Pop had started to believe that she could have any sort of success she wanted.

Mr. Player tried to get me to work at the song, but I

didn't take any notice of him. And now I'm going to have my name on a single when I don't deserve it, she told herself. *We might be able to pretend to others, but I'll always know that any success that comes from* Lollipop Lullaby *was down to Lolly, not me.*

Pop was feeling more and more miserable. At this rate, if she didn't make some effort to put things right, she'd never be able to sleep tonight. She abandoned the drink and got to her feet. She hurried back downstairs and outside. If she could catch Mr. Player before he went home, she could at least apologize to him. It would be a start.

It was quite late and Pop was afraid the teacher might have gone before she could get over to his room, so she headed for the staff car park. As soon as she saw his car, she sighed with relief. He must still be in the school. As quickly as she could, Pop ran to the main building, where Mr. Player had his room. As she turned the corner, she ran straight into him with a bump, and knocked a folder out of his hand.

"Pop!"

"Sorry. Sorry!" She kneeled down and helped him to pick up the scattered papers. "I wanted to see you," she explained as they both stood up. "To apologize."

Mr. Player laughed. He didn't seem very annoyed with her. "That's a funny way of going about it!" he told her. "What did you want to apologize for? I think I know, but you'd better tell me everything, hadn't you? Look, I'm already late," he went on. "Can we talk on the way to my car?"

Pop explained what had happened and Mr. Player nodded. "Mmm. Well, thank you for your apology, Pop. It was nice of you to come and see me so promptly."

Pop blushed. She almost wished he had been cross with her. It made it harder to bear that he was being so understanding.

"Look, we both know you've been foolish, don't we?" he went on and Pop nodded earnestly. "But I think you've learned a huge lesson, wouldn't you say?"

"Yes," Pop agreed.

"Well, that's good," he said encouragingly. "Nothing is wasted if you learn from it. Besides, it could have been even worse, with the proposed single shelved and goodness knows what. It'll be a shame if they use *Lollipop Lullaby*, but I won't be surprised if they do. It was tailor-made for you both, and record companies can be very determined to stick to what they want. The marketing people probably made the decision. Anyway, with luck, you may have got away with it, thanks to your sister."

"She did really well," said Pop in a small voice.

"Yes, she did," said Mr. Player. "She saved the day for you. And don't think I don't realize how difficult it will be if you end up having to mime to her rendition of *Lollipop Lullaby*. That will hurt a bit, won't it?"

"Yes," Pop agreed sadly. It would be *terrible*, but it would be something she'd just have to cope with.

They reached Mr. Player's car and he handed Pop his papers while he unlocked the driver's door. Pop waited while he got in and then she passed them to him. He put them on the passenger seat and paused with his hand on the door handle.

"We'll have a good go at *Lollipop Lullaby* in our

lesson tomorrow," he told her. "I know it's too late for the recording, but if it is released as a single, you'll still need to be able to do it justice in case you have to sing it live. Is that okay?"

"Yes," she told him. It wouldn't be much fun, going back over the song that would always remind her of how stupid she had been. But Mr. Player was right. She ought to make sure she could perform it faultlessly, even though it was too late for the single.

"No slacking though," he warned her. "Not if you want *me* to keep teaching you."

"No slacking," Pop agreed fervently. "And I really mean it!"

10 A Lesson Learned

Pop was as good as her word. She was a model student in every class, even in maths and science, which she hated. Her marks improved and the teachers started smiling at her again.

Pop worked even harder in her singing lessons. She did her best to put the disaster behind her and move on. She finally cracked her solo line in *Lollipop Lullaby* and honed her part until she and Lolly were in perfect harmony. The record company e-mailed more songs for them to learn and both girls studied them really hard. To Pop's relief, Satin didn't mention the recording disaster. Maybe, Pop thought, her agent had decided that she was a little to blame herself.

At any rate, the subject seemed to be closed, and a single was still planned to be released quite soon, although the twins still didn't know which song had finally been chosen.

"I do realize how lucky we are," Pop told Chloe one afternoon when they were on their way to a group singing lesson.

"I wish I had your luck," sighed Chloe. "How many singers get such amazing record deals while they're still at school?"

"Don't be envious," begged Pop. "You'll have a much longer singing career than me. And you have Manny Williams interested in you. He's one of the most respected producers in the *world*! As soon as he says you're ready, all the record companies will be falling over each other to sign you up!"

"I hope so," said Chloe. "But it's hard waiting." Pop gave her a sympathetic hug as they arrived at Mr. Player's room.

Pop always enjoyed singing lessons with the whole class. They were much more relaxed than the private lessons, when she and Lolly had to concentrate really hard.

Today, the class had fun singing an old hit together. Pop and Lolly grinned at each other as the whole class belted out the well known words. Even Danny looked as if he was enjoying himself, and singing wasn't really his thing at all. When they'd finished, Mr. Player picked up a CD and slotted it into the player.

"Before we end the lesson, I thought you'd like to hear this," he said.

Pop pricked up her ears. Occasionally, Mr. Player played something for the class to discuss, and the conversations could get quite lively as everyone liked to express an opinion, especially Pop! But as the intro swelled throughout the room, Pop put her hands to her face in horror. It was their recording! The studio must have sent a copy to the school.

Everyone was grinning and nudging each other as the CD played, but Pop wished the ground would open up and swallow her. It wasn't that the recording was bad. For an unmixed demo, it was really good. Lolly had done a great job of singing both parts. By the time the producer had created the finished article, it would be fantastic. But that was just it. *Lollipop Lullaby* had all the promise of a really big hit without Pop being a part of it. And some of the class would be sure to notice that Pop's voice was missing. Although they were twins, their voices were quite distinctive. Whatever would she say when her friends asked her why her voice wasn't on it?

Pop's face was burning. She couldn't look at anyone as the song finished, not even her sister. Then the class started applauding! Everyone really liked it, which almost made her feel worse.

"This isn't quite the finished article, is it, girls?" said Mr. Player. "It still has to be mixed."

"That's right," agreed Lolly.

"I think it's brilliant already," said Chloe enthusiastically. "Your voices are really good. What amazes me is how alike they sound. I can usually tell which one of you is singing, but I can't on that recording. I suppose they did something clever to get your voices as similar as possible. They've turned you into identical twin models with identical voices. It's a neat idea!"

Pop tried to smile at Chloe, but she felt as if she was cheating her, and that made Pop feel awful.

"So what's next?" asked Danny.

"Well, we heard yesterday that we have to go back into the studio to put the finishing touches to the recording," Lolly told him. "We still haven't met the producer who's been mixing it. Apparently, he thinks it would be good for us to be involved, which is very nice of him. I know loads of artists do have a big say in choosing the best bits of the recordings to come up with the best single possible, but we're total novices."

"Maybe that's why he wants you involved," suggested Chloe. "You have to start somewhere!"

"That's true," agreed Lolly. "Anyway, we're going again next week, but it'll only be a short visit."

"I'll tell you what the most amazing thing is about this recording," said Tara. "It's made Pop speechless!"

Everyone laughed and Lolly gave her sister a hug.

"She's just being modest," she said, and everyone laughed again.

Pop couldn't wait for the lesson to end. As soon as it was over, she rushed outside with Chloe close behind.

"There's Judge Jim!" said Pop, catching sight of the Head of the Rock Department. "I didn't realize he was back at school. Let's say hello." It would be nice to speak to him and maybe it would stop Chloe going on about the CD.

They soon caught up with the dreadlocked teacher. He was making his way carefully along the path with the aid of a stick.

"How are you?" asked Pop politely. "Is your ankle okay?"

"Not too bad," replied Judge Jim. "Still a bit weak since I broke it. Seems I'm goin' to need this stick for a while, which is annoyin'."

"At least you're back now," said Chloe.

"Sure am," he replied with a smile. "This is my first day and it feels real good. Don't let me slow you down now," he added. "I have to take my time these days."

"That's okay," said Pop brightly. "We're not in a hurry." She'd much rather chat to Judge Jim than think about the single she wasn't on.

Fortunately, Pop soon had something else to think about. The record company had decided that it would be a good idea to take some film of the twins at the recording studio for a promotional video, so she immediately started discussing clothes with her sister and the others.

"Why do they want you to dress casually?" asked Chloe, scouring the information that had been sent to the twins. "I would have thought they'd want you to dress up a bit and look glamorous!"

"They already have shots of us modelling," explained Pop. "And not many people dress up to make a recording, do they?"

"I suppose not," agreed Chloe.

"And anyway, they'll have a wardrobe person there, to check over our outfits. Even casual clothes have to look good!" explained Lolly.

Pop Diva

In spite of the excitement of being filmed, Pop hadn't forgotten about her singing. She had been practising really hard and all the songs were as perfect as they possibly could be. Even so, she was still a bit nervous as they arrived at the studio for the second time.

"I do hope Mr. Randel really *is* here this time," she told Lolly as they got out of the car. "I don't think I could face that other producer again."

She needn't have worried. Mr. Randel was there and he was really nice.

"I want to change the arrangement a little on one song, if it's okay with you," he told them. "But Jeremy Player has done a splendid job, as I knew he would. You're lucky to have him as a teacher, you know."

"We know," the twins agreed.

"By the way," he continued. "How are you at singing *Lollipop Lullaby* now, Pop?"

Pop blushed. "Fine," she assured the producer. "I thought I'd better get it right, even though the recording has been done, just in case we have to sing it to an audience some time. I'm sorry I made a mess of it before," she added.

"Don't worry," he told her. "You wouldn't be the first singer to arrive without preparing properly, and from what Jeremy Player tells me, it certainly sounds as if you're on top of things now." He picked up a letter and looked at it for a minute.

"The record company wants to release *Lollipop Lullaby* as a single in a couple of months' time," he told the girls. "So you will need to have it in your repertoire. You'll certainly have to sing it once the single comes out."

Pop and Lolly exchanged glances. Lolly couldn't hide her excitement, but she gave Pop a sympathetic smile and Pop tried her best to look happy.

"Let's run through all the songs except *Last Summer*," suggested Mr. Randel. "That's the one I want to tweak a bit, so we'll do it last. Shall we start with *Lollipop Lullaby*? Pop, could you sing your part without Lolly, so I can hear your voice properly? I'll get the engineer to feed you the recording of Lolly's voice to help you. The cameraman won't be here for ages, so we should easily be able to get all our work done before he arrives."

So Pop went through to the recording booth on her own and put the headphones on. It was a bit embarrassing for her, but she was determined not to let it affect her performance of the song. She was glad the filming would happen later. She would rather not have any distractions. After all, she had a lot to prove, and she didn't want to let Mr. Player down again.

While she waited for the engineer to find the right place on the tape, Pop grew really nervous. She didn't think she was going to enjoy singing the song one bit. But it was all right. As soon as the tune came round with Lolly's voice on it, Pop really wanted to join in. She gave the song everything she'd got and was quite pleased with her performance.

"That's great!" agreed Mr. Randel when she'd finished. "I'll be able to report back to the record company that you're note-perfect now. Excellent!"

They spent some time discussing and trying out the

little alterations Mr. Randel wanted on the last song. It was so interesting that time flew by.

"We've had a good session today," said Mr. Randel in a pleased voice. "I've got lots of material on tape to finish the mix now. I hope you think *Last Summer* is better."

"Oh yes!" the twins chorused.

They just had time to have a drink before the film people came. There was a wardrobe lady and someone to do their make-up, and it didn't take long to get Pop and Lolly ready.

The cameraman took lots of film of Pop and Lolly singing into microphones. He liked it when Pop put her headphones casually around her neck and got Lolly to do the same. Then he wanted some footage of the twins by the mixing desk. "Can you look as if you know what you're doing?" he asked.

"We do know a bit!" protested Pop.

Lolly giggled. "Like this?" she asked. She reached out her hand towards the knobs and the engineer winced.

"Not that one!" he begged. "I don't want to have to reset it."

Even so, they had fun pretending, although they *were* careful not to touch anything! Then the film people roped in Gavin Randel.

"We'd like to get a shot of you all discussing something exciting," said the woman in charge of the filming. "And then that's us finished. You don't need to worry about what you actually say because there's no sound."

Gavin Randel entered into the spirit of the occasion. He ignored the camera and drew the twins into a huddle.

"I'm going to send some more songs to Mr. Player for you to learn," he said. "Just so we've got plenty to choose from. It's good to have a selection of songs recorded because, if all goes well, the company is bound to want to look at releasing an album. What do you think about that?"

"Fantastic!" enthused Lolly, forgetting all about the camera.

A Lesson Learned

Pop had stars in her eyes too. "That *would* be exciting!" she agreed. Somehow, her voice not being on the single didn't seem to matter quite so much now. Pop was still part of the whole dizzy experience. "Everything seems to be happening so fast," she said.

"You wait." Mr. Randel laughed. "I hope you're ready, because if *Lollipop Lullaby* is a success you'll be incredibly busy. There'll be live appearances, parties, openings and you'll be asked to sing the song wherever you go! How about that?"

"How *about* that!" exclaimed the twins. "Mega cool!"

11 A Busy Time

It was a very busy time at school too. Everyone was rehearsing frantically for the school concert as well as trying to keep up with their academic work. It was even harder for Pop and Lolly with the extra work they had to do for the record company. But with Mr. Player's help, they managed to squeeze in some time to learn the new songs as well as doing everything else.

"Why don't you sing *Lollipop Lullaby* at the concert?" suggested Mr. Player one morning. "It would be great for the school to see you performing something that is going to be a big hit."

"I'm not sure it'll be *that* big a hit!" Lolly laughed modestly. "But it's a good idea, isn't it, Pop?"

"Yes, why not?" agreed Pop. "It's the most tricky of those we've recorded so far, but I feel really confident singing it now. Who knows, it might just win us some Rising Stars points. Let's do it!"

Everyone in the school had heard of Pop and Lolly's soon-to-be-released single and wanted to know more about it.

"Is it true that it was written especially for you?" asked an older girl called Rosie, as she was passing Pop and Lolly in the lunch queue one day.

"Yes, it was," Pop told her. "We're very lucky."

"What's it called?" she asked.

"*Lollipop Lullaby*," Lolly told her.

"The lyrics are wonderful!" butted in Marmalade, who had been listening shamelessly to the conversation. "The chorus goes like this."

He moved out of the queue and struck a pose. "*With a sprinkle of Lolly*." He pretended to sprinkle something over Lolly's head. "*And a sparkle of Pop*." He threw his arms wide, almost knocking the tray out of a passing student's hand. "Oops. Sorry!" he said and stopped messing about.

"Don't take any notice of his teasing," Rosie advised Pop and Lolly seriously. "A song so personal to you could become your hallmark. It could turn you into famous singers and make sure you're well known for years. Congratulations!"

"Thank you," said Lolly. She linked arms with her sister. "We do know how lucky we are, don't we, Pop?"

"We certainly do," Pop agreed. She gave Lolly a quick hug. More than anything, she knew how lucky she was to have a sister like Lolly. Not once had she moaned or grumbled at the mistakes Pop had made over *Lollipop Lullaby*. She'd done her best all the way through to help Pop and it wasn't her fault that Pop's voice wouldn't be on the single. Pop knew her secret was safe with Lolly too. Her loyalty made Pop feel humble, and very lucky indeed!

A few days before the school concert, a small parcel came for Pop and Lolly. They took it up to their room and Lolly opened it.

"What is it?" asked Chloe as Lolly pulled off the wrapping.

"Wow!" cried Lolly excitedly. "Look at this, Pop! It's the finished CD of our single."

"Let's have a look," said Chloe and Tara together. They scrambled over their beds and joined Lolly on hers.

"And there's a note from Mr. Randel," Lolly added. "*Here are a couple of copies of the final mix,*" she read. "*I hope you both approve. You'll be getting a letter soon about plans for the launch day. Keep your voices ready and look out your best dresses!*"

"Wow!" said Chloe. "Isn't it *exciting*? I'm so thrilled for you both. I'm going to get a copy as soon as it's out. And I can't wait to see the video online."

"Put the CD on then," said Tara. "Let's hear what the final version is like. I wonder if it's been changed much from the first mix we heard."

Pop didn't really want to hear the final version of the song. She had done well at putting the past behind her, but now the CD was actually in her hand, her failure to make it onto the recording was rather hard to take.

She studied the insert anxiously. It wasn't the finished design. There was no picture of the twins on the front or any artwork, but there was a list of the people involved in producing the song. Pop read down the list anxiously. She had been afraid that her name wouldn't appear, but there it was, alongside Lolly's. It made sense from a marketing point of view, and Pop knew that her sister wouldn't mind, but Pop felt awkward about it. Although she was relieved, it was difficult seeing her name there and knowing she didn't deserve any of the credit.

"You put it on," she suggested to Lolly, "and I'll go and make a celebratory drink for us all."

"All right," agreed Lolly understandingly. "I'll put it on in a moment."

But Chloe had already slotted the CD into the player and as Pop reached the door she could hear the opening bars. She went out into the corridor and tried not to listen, but it was hopeless. She knew the song so well, every note was burned into her brain. In another couple of bars, Lolly would sing Pop's solo line and Pop didn't know how she would be able to bear it.

She reached the kitchen and went to the sink. Water rushed noisily into the kettle but she could still hear the music. And then she hurriedly turned off the tap and stood there in amazement. It was *her*! Pop's voice was coming out of the player, singing the solo. Then she became unsure. *Was* it her or was it her imagination?

She put the kettle down and went back into the corridor. She wasn't mistaken. There they were, singing the next verse together. It was definitely both of their voices, not just Lolly's. But how? And then Pop realized. Mr. Randel must have been recording her voice when she sang *Lollipop Lullaby* for him at the last recording session, and he had decided it was good enough to go into the final mix.

Pop felt near to tears. She'd been so sure that she'd blown it, but Mr. Randel had given her another chance. She would remember this for her whole life and always be grateful to him. All Pop's worries and troubles over the past few weeks were at an end. *Both* of their voices had made it onto the single!

The song was coming to an end and Lolly appeared in the corridor. She looked as thrilled as Pop. The final chorus was coming round and the twins couldn't resist it. They simply had to join in with themselves!

"With a smile from Lolly."

Lolly held out her arms towards Pop.

"And a shimmy from Pop."

Pop ran to her sister and they gave each other a huge hug.

"It's a Lollipop Lullaby!"

✳ So you want
to be a pop star?

✳

Turn the page to read some top tips
on how to make your dreams
✳ come true... ✳

✳ Making it in the music biz ✳

Think you've got tons of talent?
Well, music maestro Judge Jim Henson,
Head of Rock at top talent academy Rockley
Park, has put together his hot tips to help
you become a superstar…

✳ Number One Rule: Be positive!
You've got to believe in yourself.

✳ Be active! Join your school choir
or form your own band.

✳ Be different! Don't be afraid to stand
out from the crowd.

✳ Be determined! Work hard and stay focused.

✳ Be creative! Try writing your own material –
it will say something unique about you.

✳ Be patient! Don't give up if things
don't happen overnight.

 Be ready to seize opportunities
when they come along.

Be versatile! Don't have a one-track mind – try out new things and gain as many skills as you can.

 Be passionate! Don't be afraid to show some emotion in your performance.

Be sure to watch, listen and learn all the time.

Be willing to help others. You'll learn more that way.

Be smart! Don't neglect your school work.

 Be cool and don't get big-headed! Everyone needs friends, so don't leave them behind.

Always stay true to yourself.

And finally, and most importantly, enjoy what you do!

 Go for it! It's all up to you now...

Usborne Quicklinks

For links to exciting websites where you can find out more about becoming a pop star and even practise your singing with online karaoke, go to the Usborne Quicklinks Website at www.usborne-quicklinks.com and enter the keywords fame school.

Internet safety

When using the Internet make sure you follow these safety guidelines:

 Ask an adult's permission before using the Internet.

 Never give out personal information, such as your name, address or telephone number.

 If a website asks you to type in your name or e-mail address, check with an adult first.

 If you receive an e-mail from someone you don't know, do not reply to it.

For more

read these other
fabulous books...

Reach for the Stars

Chloe wants to be a star...

Chloe totally loves singing and spends hours practising in her bedroom, miming into her hairbrush in front of thousands of imaginary fans. So when she gets the chance to audition for Rockley Park – the school for wannabe pop stars – Chloe's determined to make the grade. But first she has to persuade her parents that her ambition is for real. She knows it's going to be tough, but life in the music biz isn't all glitz and glamour.

Will Chloe get to live her dream?

9870746061176
£3.99

Rising Star

Get ready for the next singing sensation!

Chloe's made it into top talent academy Rockley Park, her first step on the road to success as a pop singer. She's desperate to perform in the school's Rising Stars concert – she's heard that talent scouts often turn up from the big record companies – but she's got one problem...she can't find her voice! Chloe's friends rally round and try to help get the power back in her voice, but time is running out.

Will Chloe miss her Big Chance?

9870746061183
£3.99

Secret Ambition

Lights, camera, action!

A TV crew is coming to Rockley Park school and model twins Pop 'n' Lolly are the star attraction. The talented twosome are used to doing everything together and they make the perfect double act. So Pop can't understand why Lolly seems so fed up.

Will Pop discover Lolly's secret before she ruins their glittering career?

9780746061206
£3.99

Rivals!

The competition is hot!

Danny's a truly talented drummer and he's in constant demand at Rockley Park school for the stars. But Charlie, the other drummer in his year, is jealous of Danny's success. Tension mounts between the two rivals so when they're forced to play together in the school concert sparks could fly!

They've got everything to play for, but who will come out on top?

9780746061190
£3.99

Tara's Triumph

Tara really rocks!

Tara is following her dream of becoming a rock star. But when she hears about an African school for orphans she decides that raising money is more important than her ambitions. A charity CD seems like a great idea as she's surrounded by talented friends and famous teachers at Rockley Park, school for the stars.

Will Tara succeed or will she get herself into more trouble than she bargained for?

9780746068359
£3.99

Lucky Break

He's in the spotlight!

Marmalade – named after his bright orange hair – is one of the best dancers at Rockley Park, the school for up-and-coming stars. But he's also the class clown, and things gets out of hand when a new boy arrives and Marmalade starts to show off even more than usual. It looks as though he's heading for a fall – literally!

Could this really be Marmalade's lucky break?

9870746068366
£3.99

Solo Star

It's time for Rising Stars!

The Rising Stars concert is the highlight of the year at talent school Rockley Park. Chloe is desperate to take part – the show is going to be on TV and this could be her big break! So she's thrilled when she hears she's made the grade. The only trouble is she has to perform with a band, when she's always wanted to be a solo star.

Will Chloe be able to shine onstage?

9780746073032
£3.99

Christmas Stars

Everyone wants to be a Christmas star!

Talent school Rockley Park is buzzing with festive fun. Chloe and her friends are rehearsing for the Christmas concert and desperately want to impress their favourite teacher, Judge Jim. They've even planned a secret surprise for him. But then there's some shocking news, and it seems he won't make the concert after all.

Can everyone pull together to make Judge Jim's Christmas really sparkle?

9780746077429
£3.99

And look out for

Battle of the Bands

An international battle of the bands competition for fame schools like Rockley Park is announced, and Chloe and her friends are thrilled to be taking part!

9780746078839

£3.99

Coming soon...

Cindy Jefferies' varied career has included being a Venetian-mask maker and a video DJ. Cindy decided to write *Fame School* after experiencing the ups and downs of her children, who have all been involved in the music business. Her insight into the lives of wannabe pop stars and her own musical background means that Cindy knows how exciting and demanding the quest for fame and fortune can be.

Cindy lives on a farm in Gloucestershire, where the animal noises, roaring tractors and rehearsals of Stitch, her son's indie-rock band, all help her write!

To find out more about Cindy Jefferies, visit her website: www.cindyjefferies.co.uk

For more *inspirational* reads,
check out
www.fiction.usborne.com

And if you've enjoyed

you'll love

SUMMER CAMP
SECRETS

Fun, friendship, secrets, boys...
Summer camp has it all!

SUMMER CAMP SECRETS

Don't miss this sunny new series –
pack one in your suitcase today!

MISS MANHATTAN
City chick Natalie has a big secret to hide…
ISBN 9780746084557

PRANKSTER QUEEN
Mischievous Jenna's wild stunts get totally out of control.
ISBN 9780746084564

BEST FRIENDS?
Will Grace realize her new friend is not all she seems?
ISBN 9780746084571

LITTLE MISS NOT-SO-PERFECT
"Perfect" Alex can't bear to admit she's got a problem.
ISBN 9780746084571

BLOGGING BUDDIES
The girls support each other through their back-to-school
blues.
ISBN 9780746084601

PARTY TIME!
Will everyone still get on at the camp reunion party?
ISBN 9780746084618

All priced at £4.99